PENGUINS DON'T WEAR SWEATERS!

MARIKKA TAMURA

ILLUSTRATED BY
DANIEL RIELEY

Nancy Paulsen Books

For the penguins and the people who work
to save threatened habitats. —M.T.

For my Mum and Dad, and all of
the penguins around the world! —D.R.

NANCY PAULSEN BOOKS
an imprint of Penguin Random House LLC
375 Hudson Street
New York, NY 10014

Library of Congress Cataloging-in-Publication Data is available upon request.

Manufactured in China by RR Donnelley Asia Printing Solutions Ltd.
ISBN 9781101996966
10 9 8 7 6 5 4 3 2 1

Design by Dave Kopka.
Text set in Aptifer Slab LT Pro.
The artwork created for this book is a combination
of pencils, inks, handmade textures and digital.

Penguins on ice.

Penguins in the sea.
Penguins love the sea!

Gliding with the fish.
Slipping fast away from seals.

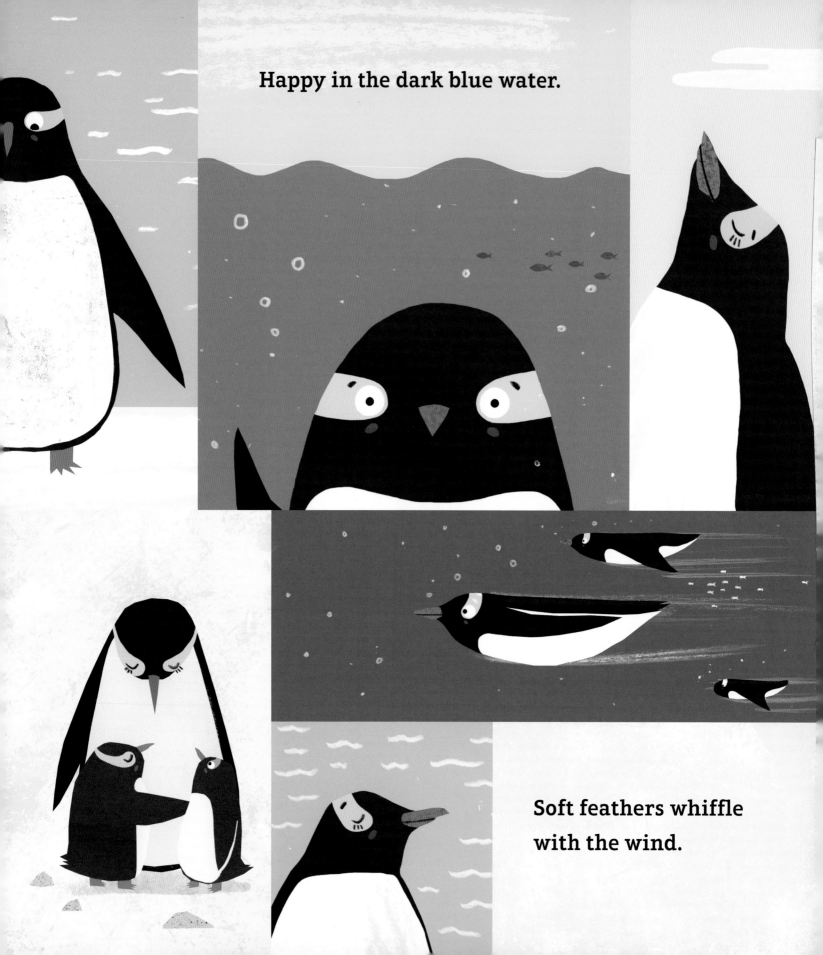

Happy in the dark blue water.

Soft feathers whiffle
with the wind.

Black and white—ORANGE feet!—against the sky.

Penguins huddling, cuddling, waddling.

Penguins doing penguin things. Diving deep.

But WHAT is this? Something is floating in the water.

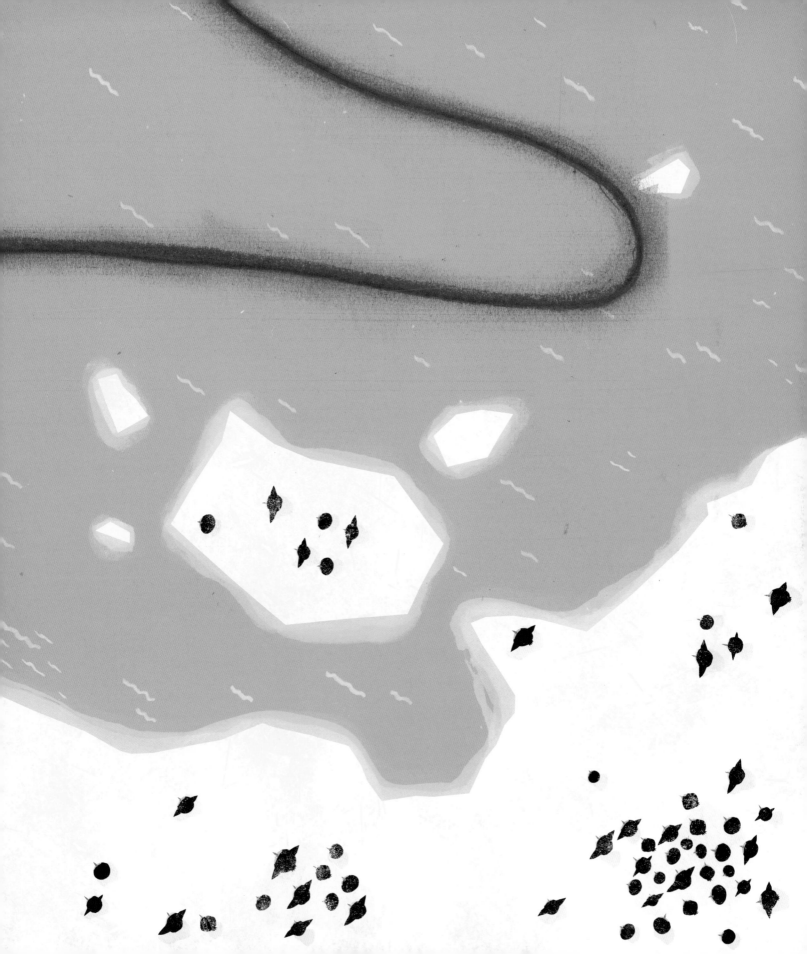

Dark. Gooey. Oily. Slick.

Across the surface of the water,
oil pools in inky puddles.

Penguins can't live in this!
It coats round bodies with goo.
It makes sleek feathers stay sticky and wet.

It smells and tastes funny.
Not nice, like fish.
Not good, like salt and sun.

Help! Penguins can't swim in this!

Can't swim. Can't fish. Can't soak up sun.

Now what? Big Boots are coming.

Many boots. Big Boots by the water's edge.

Looking at the greasy water.

At the cold, greasy penguins.

"PENGUINS NEED SWEATERS!"
Big Boots yell.

Sweaters might keep round bodies safe and warm.
Sweaters might help keep penguins
the way penguins need to be.

Big Boots everywhere knit sweaters.

They hurry and knit and send them
to help poor oily penguins.

But penguins DON'T wear sweaters!
Only NOW they do.
Big Boots bring sweaters. All kinds.
Orange like penguin feet.
Yellow like the sun.
Blue like the sky.

Some are knit in straight, even rows.
Others are more wobbly.
Look at *you*, penguin!
Wearing a sweater!

Sweaters cover black-and-white suits.
Sweaters are as warm as the sun. Almost.
A little itchy, though.

SEE! Sometimes penguins DO wear sweaters.
They pose for pictures because Big Boots
went to all that trouble.

PENGUINS WEAR
CUTE SWEATERS

When the cameras go away,
penguins slip out of their sweaters.

Helpful hands and soapy suds wash away oil and goo.

And when the coast is clear, penguins return.
They dive down deep again.
Happy to be penguins doing penguin things.

Author's Note

I first saw this story in a news feed scrolling across my computer screen. An adorable photo of penguins wearing sweaters made me pause. People around the globe were knitting sweaters to save oil-soaked little blue penguins in Phillip Island, Australia. My first thought was, *Hey, I can do that! And so can my mom and sister! We knit—we can save penguins!* But then I dug a little deeper past super-cute photos and feel-good news.

Penguins Don't Wear Sweaters! is fiction, but it has its basis in fact. Penguins covered in oil have difficulty regulating their body temperature. Although wearing a sweater *can* help keep them warm and stop them from ingesting oil as they preen, it can also have harmful effects, especially on other species of penguins. Experts from International Bird Rescue caution that sweaters are not a useful tool in rehabilitating most penguins. Sweaters press oil against their skin, trapping chemical vapors. Also, the handling involved in putting a penguin in clothing just plain stresses them out. Thus, sweater donations that have flooded in after other oil spills have gone unused. There are better ways to rehabilitate penguins, but as with many things, it's not a simple one-step fix.

It turns out I learned a lot more from that first cute photo than I expected. Not only facts about penguins but about the importance of reading *beyond* the short news bites. (And it also turns out if I had knitted a sweater for the Phillip Island penguins, the Penguin Foundation most likely would have used it on a toy penguin and sold it to raise funds to protect their habitat.)

—MARIKKA TAMURA

If you want to learn more, here are some helpful links:
International Bird Rescue: www.bird-rescue.org
Penguin Foundation: penguinfoundation.org.au